DATE DUE	
MAY 2 6 1987	JUN 2 8 1995	
JUL 0 7 1987		
JUL 2 8 1987		
DEC 0 1 1987		
DEC 2 6 1987		
JAN 1 3 1988		
JUN 0 9 1988		
JUN 3 0 1988		
JUN 2 5 1993		
JUN 2 9 1994		
SEP 0 7 1994		

MY GRANDMA'S IN A NURSING HOME

My Grandma's
in a Nursing Home

Judy Delton *and* Dorothy Tucker
Pictures by Charles Robinson

ALBERT WHITMAN & COMPANY, NILES, ILLINOIS

Also by Judy Delton
Bear and Duck on the Run
Duck Goes Fishing
The Elephant in Duck's Garden
I'll Never Love Anything Ever Again
It Happened on Thursday
Lee Henry's Best Friend
My Mom Hates Me in January
My Mother Lost Her Job Today
A Pet for Duck and Bear

by Judy Delton and Elaine Knox-Wagner
The Best Mom in the World

Library of Congress Cataloging-in-Publication Data

Delton, Judy.
  My grandma's in a nursing home.

  Summary: Jason hates his first visit to visit his
grandmother in a nursing home, but as he returns, he
finds his visits make a difference to his grandmother
and the other patients.
  [1. Nursing homes—Fiction. 2. Grandmothers—Fiction.
3. Aged—Fiction] I. Tucker, Dorothy. II. Robinson,
Charles, 1931–   ill. III. Title.
PZ7.D388Mx 1986   [Fic]   86-1640
ISBN 0-8075-5333-6

Text © 1986 by Judy Delton and Dorothy Tucker
Illustrations © 1986 by Charles Robinson
Published in 1986 by Albert Whitman & Company, Niles, Illinois
Published simultaneously in Canada by General Publishing, Limited, Toronto
All rights reserved. Printed in the United States of America.
10 9 8 7 6 5 4 3 2 1

To Kevin J.D. & D.T.
To my father C.R.

My grandma is in a nursing home called Meadowbrook.
Mom says it sounds like a cemetery.
Dad says it sounds like a golf club.
My grandma says, "I want to go home."

I want her to come home, too.
We used to work in her garden together.
She'd say, "You really have a green thumb, Jason."
Last year we picked three baskets of tomatoes
that I helped her plant.

But she can't go home because
no one is there to take care of her.
She has Alzheimer's disease, and she needs special care.

Wednesday Mom said, "We'll go to visit Grandma today. Now that she's settled, she'll be happy to see you."

"Good," I said. "I miss Grandma."

When we got to Meadowbrook, an old lady opened the door. "Here, hold these eggs," she said to me.

Her hands were empty.
"What eggs?" I said to her.

"Ssshhhh," said my mother.

We went down the hall.
There were nurses in white dresses
and people in wheelchairs.
There was a smell like food and some kind of medicine.

Grandma was lying in bed in her room.
She didn't look happy. But when she saw us, she smiled.

"Hello, James!" she said to me. (James is my dad's name.)
"I'm so glad you're here."
She reached out her hand to touch me.

"My name is Jason," I said.
"Ssshhhh," said my mother.

We sat and looked at the walls.
I held Grandma's hand. She seemed to like that.
"I want to go home," she said. "Home to my garden."

"I wish you could," said my mother with tears in her eyes.
"But it's nice here. And they take good care of you."

I got tears in my eyes, too.
Grandma was right. Her garden was nicer.

I heard a TV in a room across the hall.
When I went to look, a man in a wheelchair said,
"Pull up a chair. It's almost time for the news."

On the table by the TV were some teeth in a dish.
"I can't stay," I said.

On the way home, my mother said, "Next week we'll bring
Grandma some cookies. We'll bake them together."

"I don't want to go next week!" I said.
"I want Grandma to come home.
She doesn't know my name, and there are teeth
on tables, and that lady at the door HAD no eggs!"

"Those people are lonely," said my mother.
"They need our company.
And Grandma likes to see you."

The next week, the same lady was at the door.
"Do you like my baby?" she asked me.

I didn't say, "What baby?"
I didn't say anything.

My mom smiled.

When we got to Grandma's room, I gave her the cookies.
She gave me a kiss.

"We baked them ourselves," I said.
"Thank you, James. I love chocolate chip."

I didn't tell her my name was Jason.
"You're welcome," I told her.

"I'm glad you're here," Grandma said.

When we left, the man with the TV waved.
I looked at the table. The teeth were still in the dish.

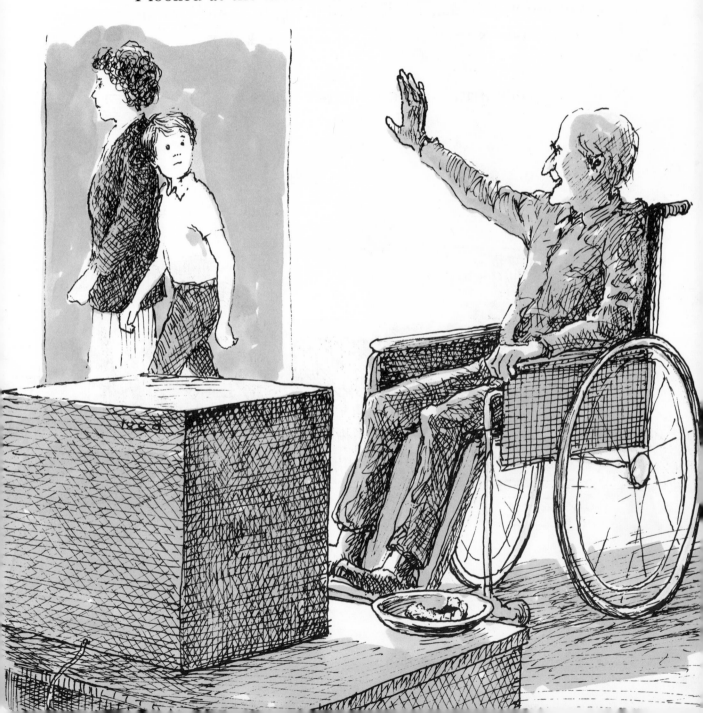

On the way home, I said, "I'm going to bring Grandma some flowers from her garden next week."

"She'll like that," said my mother.

The next week, when we got to the door, the lady wasn't there.
"Where is the lady?" I asked the nurse.

"What lady?" she said.

"The lady who asked me to hold her eggs."

"Oh, you must mean Thelma. She's at the birthday party.
You can go, too."

When we got to the dining room, Thelma was at the door.
"I have a new hat," she said, pointing to her bare head.
"Do you like it?"

"Yes," I said. "It's very nice."

I gave Grandma the flowers.
"They're from your garden.
I'm taking care of it for you."

Grandma looked puzzled,
like she'd forgotten she had a garden at all.
After a minute she said, "Thank you, James,
they're beautiful. You've always had a green thumb."

The old man who lives across the hall from Grandma
was at the party, too.
"Come here," he called.

I looked around. "Me?"

He nodded.
"I'm having trouble eating this cake without my teeth.
Could you push me to my room to get them?"

"All right," I said.
There were two handles on the wheelchair.
I pushed him to his room.
On the way he asked, "What's your name?"

"Jason," I answered. "What's yours?"
"Harry," he said.

We got the teeth. Harry put them in his mouth.
(He looked better with teeth.)
Then I pushed him back to the party.

"Come and sit with us, James," called my grandma.
She patted the chair next to her.

"Okay," I said. "Whose birthday party is it?"

"It's for everyone here whose birthday comes in August,"
said the man next to me. "I was born on the seventh.
My name is Swen Olson."

"Happy birthday, Mr. Olson!" I said.

Grandma didn't mind the party.
She sang "Happy Birthday" along with everyone else.
Then we all had cake and ice cream.
"Tonight they're going to show a movie," she said.
"I might like that."

I told her I'd come back next week.
(By then the asters should be blooming.)

When we left, I said, "That was a nice party."
My mom nodded.

"I think next week I'll bring my checkerboard
and checkers. I'll bet Harry knows how to play."

"I'll bet he does, too," said my mother.